Sheldon Lewis

More Mini Adventures in Jerusalem

Sheldon Lewis

More Mini Adventures in Jerusalem

Illustrated by Kim Howard

Hadassa Word Press

Imprint
Any brand names and product names mentioned in this book are subject to trademark, brand or patent protection and are trademarks or registered trademarks of their respective holders. The use of brand names, product names, common names, trade names, product descriptions etc. even without a particular marking in this work is in no way to be construed to mean that such names may be regarded as unrestricted in respect of trademark and brand protection legislation and could thus be used by anyone.

Cover image: Provided by the author

Publisher:
Hadassa Word Press
is a trademark of
International Book Market Service Ltd., member of OmniScriptum Publishing Group
17 Meldrum Street, Beau Bassin 71504, Mauritius

Printed at: see last page
ISBN: 978-620-2-45500-8

*Dedicated to my beloved grandchildren
Gabriel, Sari, Nathan, Maya, Noah, Ava,
Rachel, Lev, and Michael
who inspire me everyday with their open hearts
to imagine a world without hatred and bigotry.*
— *Sheldon Lewis*

*Dedicated to my daughter, Amelia Howard
who is my greatest teacher.*
— *Kim Howard*

∽ ABOUT THE ILLUSTRATOR ∽

Children's book illustrator, textile designer, and fount of energy, Kim Howard has been a professional full-time artist and teacher for over 25 years. Formally trained under painters Joan Brown and Elmer Bishoff at UC Berkeley, and at the San Francisco Academy of Art College, Kim launched her artistic career through various stints at Berkeley Repertory Theatre (where she developed an insatiable love of drama), and in textile design at The Gap and Esprit. She has illustrated 22 children's books and taught painting workshops around the world. Her great loves are her daughter Amelia, wild animals and habitats, travel, to be strong and healthy, and cooking. Before her 100th birthday, Kim hopes to live in a fantastic treehouse, high in the sky.

∽ ABOUT THE CONTRIBUTING ∽ ILLUSTRATOR

Sari Lewis is a teenager who loves art and animals. She is a specialist at drawing animals! The images she contributed of the two boys aboard the donkey at the beginning and at the conclusion of the book mark her public debut as an illustrator. She is also a beloved granddaughter of the author.

∾ ABOUT THE AUTHOR ∾

Sheldon Lewis has been a community rabbi for almost 50 years. He has always been drawn to young children, to their spirit, their imaginations, and their honesty. He began composing stories for kids when his own children were young. Under the tutelage of his revered teacher, Dr. Abraham Joshua Heschel of blessed memory, he absorbed a passion for peacemaking. He is the author of *Mini Adventures in Jerusalem*, and he now adds a sequel with the same miniature heroes. These stories represent his attempt to teach peacemaking to kids in a way they can understand. He has felt the pain of the Israel-Arab conflict very deeply, and these collections of stories are intended to open the hearts of a new generation to a vision of peace. He is also the author of *Torah of Reconciliation* and *Bridging Word and World*. Married to Lorri, they have been blessed with four sons, four daughters-in-law and nine grandchildren.

∾∾

～ TABLE OF CONTENTS ～

∾ INTRODUCTION ∾

Welcome back to the adventures of Mati and Ahmed! The stories that follow continue the sometimes wild experiences of two very small boys who met at the Western Wall in Jerusalem. These boys are the same size, the size of a thumb; but they come from very different backgrounds. Mati is Jewish; Ahmed is a Muslim. They study at different schools, learn from different holy books, and go to pray at a synagogue and at a mosque. Their friendship has grown as they learn about each other, and they find that they share many values. Do you remember how they were rescued from a big burlap sack of sesame seeds, saved a donkey who was running loose in the *suk* (market place), helped a very poor beggar woman when her coins spilled onto a busy sidewalk, rescued a poor injured kitten in a park, and shared time together in a synagogue and a mosque while doing good deeds for others in need?

Now prepare yourself for more very wild rides with these two boys. Wherever they go, they are in for unexpected adventures, sometimes even danger. And they are learning how special it is to be friends with someone who is different.

∼ FINDING EACH OTHER *AGAIN* ∼ AT THE WALL

Mati and Ahmed first met in a crevice in the Western Wall in Jerusalem. The space they had found between two gigantic stones was just big enough for the two thumb-sized boys, and it provided cover from the rain that day. Meeting in their "cave" for the first time was the beginning of a special friendship. How could they imagine that one day the Wall would help them once again?!

Now they were going back to the *suk,* the Arab market place in the Old City of Jerusalem. It was always a treat. The two boys had once made a new friend there for life when they rescued a donkey who had broken loose and was lost and frightened in the crowded narrow pathways. Actually they made two new friends: the donkey and its master, Mahmood.

"Whenever you come back here, boys, I promise you a ride on my donkey!" Mahmood had said. "After all, it's safer for you being up high rather than scurrying around at peoples' feet!"

Today Mati and Ahmed took advantage of Mahmood's offer, and soon they were atop the donkey as he led them deeper and deeper into the suk. They had no special plans. They just loved the noise, the crowds, and the fragrance of spices in the marketplace.

It seemed to the boys that the donkey liked having them aboard, too. Mati suggested they name him *Yakir*, dear one.

"Do you think he remembers us?" asked Mati.

"Oh, yes! I think *Yakir* is smiling at us," exclaimed Ahmed.

"Look, Ahmed," said Mati, pointing to a woman with a basket of large, circular pita breads balanced on her head.

"I wish I could have a bite!" answered Ahmed.

Mahmood overheard the boys, and soon they each had a big piece of fresh pita, still warm from the oven.

Laughing and chewing, the boys admired the different head coverings that people wore as they passed by. There were big round fur hats and black hats with wide brims on many Jewish men as well as knitted *kipot*. There were *kaffiyas* of many colors on the heads of Arab men and veils covering the hair and sometimes the faces of Muslim women. Scarves concealed the hair of some of the Jewish women.

It was such fun watching people and the happenings in the *suk*. Many of the storekeepers already knew Mati and Ahmed from before and waved to them as they passed:

"Ahalan v'sahalan, boys. Welcome!" they would hear. And the boys would always wave back.

Sometimes another donkey would pass them

going the opposite way. In narrow pathways, that could be exciting.

It could also be dangerous.

While they were looking in one direction, a donkey laden with big baskets passed by on their other side. The baskets were so wide that they reached where the boys were sitting on a blanket on Yakir's back, and the boys were suddenly knocked off their perch! Mati and Ahmed found themselves tumbling off the donkey. Instinctively, they grabbed at whatever they could, at the edges of the blanket, at the donkey's hair, even at a passersby's robe or shirt. They were separated from each other as they tumbled towards the ground. Everything happened so quickly that Mahmood wasn't even aware that the boys were no longer riding on the donkey's back!

Clutching at anything they could, they soon found themselves on the ground, dodging the passing shoes and shouting out to Mahmood and to each other. They lost sight of each other; but, fortunately, they were not hurt. The noise on the street was so loud that their small voices could not be heard. Each of them tried to find a place on the side of the pathway where it would be safe for a very small boy. As much as they looked and called out, they could not find each other.

"Ahmed, I'm here. Where are you?" Mati groaned. No answer.

The crowds were moving briskly, and the two boys had no choice but to be carried along with them. Hopping on shoes for a ride, each of them kept hoping to run into the other. At times, they would climb up to a higher place to have a better view, trying to see each other or, at least, Mahmood's donkey.

"I've got to find my friend," Ahmed thought to himself, but there was no sign of Mati.

Separately, Ahmed and Mati traveled further and further into the *suk*. They were tired and discouraged.

Suddenly Mati caught sight of something very familiar, the large plaza in front of the *kotel,* the Wall. With a burst of energy, he ran towards the Wall. Now he knew what he must do. As he approached the Wall, he found a small scrap of paper, took out a tiny pencil from his pocket, and he began to write his prayer:

Dear God,
I lost my friend Ahmed. Please help me find him!

Mati folded his prayer again and again to make it smaller and then climbed into a small space between the huge stones. Placing his paper prayer beside him, he lay down. His fall from the donkey, the effort he had made to find Ahmed, and the sadness he felt combined to make him very tired. It wasn't long before he slept.

Mati did not know how long he had been asleep when he was awakened by the sound of another piece of paper being shoved into the very crevice where he lay. It was someone else's prayer! And it opened just enough for him to take a glimpse. He could barely make out some words: *Please help me find....* Usually no one would dare to open someone else's prayer. But Mati could not resist. He pulled at the folded paper, and then he read: *Allah, please help me find my friend, Mati!*

Ahmed had learned about the Wall from Mati, and he knew about the prayers that many people wrote to God when they were in need.

Mati jumped up and looked out from his small "cave". He could not believe his eyes! There outside stood Ahmed facing the Wall!

"Ahmed!" yelled Mati. "It's you!! Here I am!"

"Mati," Ahmed screamed excitedly. "It's you! I looked and looked, and here you are."

Mati climbed out of the Wall; and there, in front of many people, they hugged each other.

"This Wall is special," Ahmed said. "I think it makes miracles."

⁓ WELCOMING THE STRANGER ⁓

Tel Aviv is a beautiful city by the sea not far from Jerusalem. There are tall buildings, wide streets with interesting shops lining them, and busy people going every which way. Ahmed's parents had errands in Tel Aviv, and they invited Mati to join their family. While the grownups were busy, the boys could explore on their own.

Mati and Ahmed were excited. They walked down Dizengoff Avenue, one of the main streets in the city, dodging the feet of passersby. Then they decided to take a ride together on the worn sandal of a young man who was walking very fast.

They jumped together onto his shoe as his foot hit the sidewalk.

"Hold tight onto the strap, Ahmed," Mati called out as he saw Ahmed slipping.

"I've got his buckle!" answered Ahmed.

The two boys loved the ride as the man's shoe went up and down as he walked. It was better than going on rides at an amusement park!

While the two boys were hanging on, they noticed that the man's foot was dark black. So was his ankle and as much of his leg that they could see. He was a man with black skin. They also noticed that his pants were torn.

Soon the man turned into a building and went up the stairs to an office where he was welcomed by another man. He had no idea that two small boys were still clinging to his shoe.

"*Shalom,* please sit down," said the man. "What is your name?"

"I am Abdo," answered the black man.

"I understand that you have just arrived at our border from Africa."

"Yes, I come from Sudan, and I walked a long way across the desert with my wife and small child."

"Why have you come to Israel?"

"I feared that my family and I would be hurt. Some of my relatives have disappeared. It was very dangerous for us to stay there."

"Abdo, you will be safe here in Israel. Here are some papers for you to fill out. There is a table in the next room. Please bring the papers back to me when you finish."

Mati and Ahmed listened quietly.

"Look at his torn pants," Ahmed whispered.

"And his worn-out sandals," answered Mati also is a whisper. "He must be very poor."

Abdo stood, and walked to the next room, sitting down by the table.

"Abdo!" the boys called out together.

Abdo heard their voices but did not know from where they came.

"We are down here on your sandal!" Mati said.

Was Abdo surprised when he looked down to see two small boys clinging to the strap on his sandal. "Who are you, and how did you get onto my shoe?"

Ahmed answered: "My name is Ahmed, and my friend is Mati. We jumped aboard on your shoe for a ride on Dizengoff Street."

13

Abdo bent down and picked up Mati and Ahmed, and exclaimed: "I've never seen boys your size."

The boys, now seeing Abdo eye to eye, realized that he was a very tall man. His color was very black, and his eyes were dark, too. His black hair was uncombed, some strands of hair falling over his face.

"Maybe this is the first meeting ever between a very tall man and two very small boys!" Abdo exclaimed.

"We heard how you got here, walking across the desert," Mati said. "It must have been very dangerous."

"Yes, there was very little water and few places to find shelter from the heat and few safe places to sleep at night," answered Abdo.

"We live in Jerusalem, Abdo," ventured Ahmed. "We can help you!"

"Wow!," said Abdo. "My family have been very lonely since coming to Israel. You will be our first friends!"

Abdo continued: "But I have a problem right now. I do not know how to read or write, and I need to fill out this form."

Mati and Ahmed said in one voice: "We know how to write!"

Soon the two boys stood on the desktop with the paper before them. They together took hold of a pen they found nearby. It took the two of them to hold it upright with Mati near the point and Ahmed with his arms stretched over his head, holding up the back of the pen.

"We'll ask you questions, Abdo," said the boys, "and you tell us the answers. We already know your name."

Immediately the boys wrote his name on the form.

"Do you have a last name?"

15

"No, just Abdo."

"What is your wife's name?"

"She is Uduru, and our baby is Minoo."

The boys soon had filled in all of the spaces on the form, including Abdo's story of where they came from, why the family had left their home, and all of the troubles they had on the way to the border of Israel.

"Why do you want to stay in Israel?" the boys read the last question on the form.

"It is hard to be away from my own country, but I want a safe place to live, to work, and to take care of Minoo."

Abdo began to cry as he answered this last question. Mati and Ahmed felt tears forming in their own eyes.

With the form now finished, Abdo rose, placed the boys on his shoulder, and gave the completed form to the man in the next room.

As they walked out onto the street, Ahmed offered, "Come with us to meet my parents."

Soon Mati and Ahmed standing on Abdo's shoulders directed him to the meeting place they had discussed.

Ahmed's parents, Khalil and Mariam, were so surprised to see their son and Mati coming toward them on the shoulder of a very tall African man.

"*Salaam!*" they said, extending their hands to him.

"This is Abdo," Ahmed said. The two boys couldn't talk fast enough as they explained how they had met Abdo and told his family's story.

"We are proud of you boys," said Khalil. "We always taught Ahmed to be welcoming to strangers. We know that Mati learned the same lesson. When can we have you and your family for a meal at our home in Jerusalem?"

"I am so grateful," said Abdo. "It's the first invitation we have received."

One week later, Mati and Ahmed waited at a bus stop in Jerusalem as Abdo and his family stepped down from their bus.

"Welcome to Jerusalem!" they said in unison.

Soon they were all sitting at the table of Ahmed's family. Mati's parents had also been invited.

The baby, Minoo, stared at the two boys with her

big, dark eyes.

Mati and Ahmed made funny faces, tossed a small ball, and played peek-a-boo as the baby laughed and clapped her hands.

The boys' parents did everything possible to make this new family feel at home. Mariam even found a recipe for *asseeda*, a thick Sudanese soup which she served. The adults wanted to know everything about each other.

Soon Mati and Ahmed's families were making regular trips to a very small apartment in Tel Aviv, carrying home-made meals, kitchen pots and pans, a high chair, and even bus passes to Abdo and Uduru. The boys carried toys and used books for Minoo they no longer needed.

"Why are you doing this?" asked Abdo.

"We learn we should take care of the stranger in the Torah," Mati spoke up.

"It's the same in the *Quran!*" Ahmed added.

The boys' parents smiled with pride.

"This is an amazing country, and you are amazing people!" Uduru said with her husband Abdo nodding in agreement. "We are beginning to feel at home!"

⤳ RIDING A SQUIRREL TO SAFETY ⤳

"What is that?" asked Ahmed, pointing to a bright yellow fruit and a palm branch with leaves of other plants attached lying on a table in Mati's dining room.

"Oh, that's our *lulav* and *etrog!*" Mati answered. "Let me show you."

Mati led Ahmed to a special ladder for thumb sized boys on which they climbed onto the table -top and stood next to the *lulav* and *etrog.* "We use them on the holiday of Sukkot to thank God for fruit and all that grows. The *etrog* is like a lemon, and it smells so good. Here, take a sniff."

Ahmed put his nose up to the fruit. "Wow! I like it!"

Mati pointed to the *lulav.* "The big long branch is from a palm tree. And the small branches are from myrtle and willow bushes. Would you like to come again to the synagogue to see how we use them?"

"I sure would!" Ahmed said excitedly.

The very next day, Ahmed was sitting with Mati next to Mati's *abba* in their synagogue. He eagerly watched as Mati's father held up the *lulav* and *etrog* with two hands, said a blessing in Hebrew, and then shook them in all directions!

Mati whispered to Ahmed: "This shows that God is everywhere!"

"Oh, cool!" Ahmed responded.

The prayer service began with Mati concentrating on his miniature *siddur,* his book of prayers. Ahmed watched attentively.

After a few minutes, Ahmed turned to Mati and whispered urgently: "Did you see the squirrel up near the ceiling?"

Ahmed pointed, and Mati could

not believe his eyes. Sure enough, he saw a squirrel clinging to the wall behind the ark of the Torah where the wall touches the ceiling. The squirrel seemed frozen, not moving a muscle.

"It must have come in through an open door, climbed the wall, and then become totally scared!" whispered Mati.

"Poor squirrel!" offered Ahmed. "Is there any way we can help it find its way back outside?"

Both boys were silent, thinking.

"I do have an idea, Ahmed. Will you help me?" Mati asked.

Before Ahmed could answer, Mati began to climb up on his father's clothing with Ahmed right behind him. His *abba* had just taken hold of the *lulav* and *etrog* with both hands and was holding them up high.

Mati grabbed at a belt buckle, then a button, and even his *abba's* beard as he went higher and higher. He knew he had to act fast. Ahmed followed. Mati then jumped onto a shoulder and ran up his *abba's* arm toward the tall *lulav* without his father even being aware of the two boys.

Ahmed didn't know the plan, but he was right on Mati's heels. Mati then began to climb the *lulav*! Soon the two boys, with arms and legs wrapped around the palm branch, were really out on a limb!!

Mati knew that any second his *abba* would begin to shake the *lulav* vigorously in all directions. It was time to act on his plan. The *lulav* shaking began, and Mati and Ahmed held on tightly so they would not fall. But when *abba* shook the branch *forward* three times, Mati let go at just the right time, calling to Ahmed to do

the same. The force of the shaking propelled the two boys high into the air. Now Ahmed understood the plan! They were flying towards the squirrel!

No one in the congregation was aware of the drama happening high above. Everyone was concentrating on their prayers as they shook their *lulavim.* The boys flew through the air silently, and everything was happening very quickly.

They knew they could aim their bodies toward the squirrel. And steering themselves skillfully, they made a perfect gentle landing on the back of the squirrel with Mati up front and Ahmed right behind him.

The squirrel was so frightened and seemed to be frozen in place. Never had anyone sat on its back before. Mati and Ahmed spoke softly: "Nice squirrel! Good squirrel! We are your friends. Do not be afraid. We've come to help!"

The squirrel turned its head slightly to see its two riders. It was startled and still afraid, but slowly it relaxed as the two boys gently patted its sides.

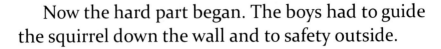

Now the hard part began. The boys had to guide the squirrel down the wall and to safety outside.

"Giddy-up!" Mati called out.

"Giddy-up!" Ahmed repeated.

The squirrel had never heard those words before, but it seemed to understand that it was time to move.

By shifting their bodies to one side or the other, the two boys found they could steer the squirrel. With its claws firmly holding onto the wall, it began to turn downward.

The men and women in the congregation were so immersed in their prayers that they did not see the strangest of sights unfolding on the wall behind the Ark of the Torah. As the squirrel turned and climbed downward, it picked up speed. Mati and Ahmed became terrified and began to shriek.

Now everyone was startled when they looked up and saw the squirrel jumping from the wall onto the *bimah* platform where the Ark was placed. A squirrel is rarely found in the synagogue and even more rare would be two tiny boys on its back!

The squirrel now saw the open door at the rear and began to run even faster with Mati and Ahmed hanging on by their fingernails. They passed Mati's *abba* who could barely blurt out, "Hang on, boys!"

"Whoaaaaa!" yelled Mati, trying to slow the speeding squirrel.

There was a tree in the outside courtyard of the synagogue, and the squirrel sensed that it was nearly home.

After running through the open door, the squirrel was back in its own world again. It rushed towards the tree, climbing instantly up the trunk and finally resting on a branch.

The boys were breathless after their harrowing ride but were still hanging on. The squirrel once again turned its head looking back at Mati and Ahmed as though inviting them to dismount.

"Let's go, Ahmed," Mati called out as he now jumped onto the branch. Ahmed quickly followed. Looking around, they saw other squirrels standing close-by watching two small boys who had helped their friend.

Abba and others came running into the courtyard to check on the two boys. They were amazed to see them standing on a branch high above them. "Mati," *Abba* called out. "How did you manage to ride the squirrel? I was so worried you would fall off!"

"*Abba*, we saw that poor squirrel stuck on the wall. We had to do something," Mati answered, still trying to catch his breath.

"OK, boys, now how can we get you down safely?" *Abba* asked.

"Can you hold up that branch one more time? What do you call it again?" Ahmed asked.

"Oh, the *lulav*!" *Abba* knew right away.

Abba held the *lulav* high as he stood on his tip toes, as high as he could reach. It just touched the bough of the tree where Mati and Ahmed stood.

"Great idea, Ahmed!" Mati said, as the two boys took hold of the pointed top and shimmied down the *lulav*.

Soon they were standing on *abba's* shoulder.

When they looked up into the tree, they saw their new squirrel friend surrounded by an entire family of squirrels, all looking down and buzzing at the gathering below.

And it seemed to Mati and Ahmed that the squirrels were trying to say "thank you".

Abba offered. "Doing one *mitzvah* can lead to another *mitzvah*. When I was doing the *mitzvah* of shaking the *lulav*, you boys used the *lulav* to fly to the rescue of a poor frightened animal. Well done!"

Ahmed turned to Mati: "Your synagogue is always a place for great adventures. What's next?!"

∼ DOING HOMEWORK ∼

Mati and Ahmed made plans. But of course, they had homework to do first.

"Bring your books to my house," Ahmed told Mati on the phone. "Then we can go play in the field down the block."

"OK," replied Mati. "I'll bring my soccer ball."

Soon the two boys were sitting at a very low table made especially for thumb-sized kids. Their books were open before them. The books were much smaller than usual. Otherwise how could they carry them in their backpacks?

"What are you studying?" asked Mati as he looked over at Ahmed's book written in Arabic.

"My teacher taught us something really great today from the Quran, and we are supposed to memorize it!"

"Can I test you?" Mati wondered aloud.

"Well, I think I know it by heart. Let me try!"

Whoever kills a soul, it is as if he had killed all people entirely. And whoever saves one – it is as if he had saved all people entirely.

"Perfect!" Mati exclaimed. "You will pass your test for sure! Is this really from the *Quran*?" Mati continued after a pause. "This sounds just like something I learned in my school from my book of the *Mishnah*! Let me show you."

Mati opened his backpack and looked through a stack of papers. Finally, he smiled as he took one page out. "Here it is!" And then he began to read:

Whoever destroys one life, the Torah considers it as though he had destroyed an entire world. And whoever saves one life, the Torah considers it as though he had saved an entire world.

"Wow!! Almost the same words!" Ahmed answered. "How could that happen?"

"Maybe because the teaching is so important God wanted *everyone* to know it!" Mati suggested.

"What did your teacher tell you about these lessons?" inquired Mati.

"She explained that each person is different from any other person who has ever lived. No two people

are exactly alike. Faces
are different, voices
are different, and
so much more
is unlike
anyone else.
And every
person is
precious
because
no one can
take his or
her place. So...
each person is like
a whole world!" Ahmed
answered.

"I remember my rabbi telling us that we learn this from the first human being, Adam, in the Torah. All the other plants and animals came into the world in great numbers. But Adam was formed all by himself to teach us that each person is like an entire world!" Mati added.

"Can you teach me these lessons from your book?" Ahmed asked. "I want to tell my teacher."

"Yes, if you will help me learn these lessons from the *Quran*. I want to tell my teacher, too!"

Soon the boys were ready to go outside.

"*Umm*, Mati and I are going out," Ahmed called to his mom. "We'll be back soon."

"Have fun, boys," she answered. "Make sure you are back before dark."

Ahmed led Mati down the stairs from his apartment to the street.

Soon they were playing in the park, kicking the soccer ball back and forth.

Not long afterwards, they heard a very loud screech from the nearby street followed by another loud bang. They looked up and saw that a car had crashed into a tree next to the park. A limb from the tree had fallen on top of the car. The boys ran as fast as they could towards the car. Soon they saw that a woman was trapped inside and she seemed to be badly hurt. She was crying out for help.

No one else was around. They had to help. They saw that the window on the driver's side was open just a crack, perhaps just big enough for two tiny boys to get inside.

"Let's try to reach the window," Ahmed yelled out.

Immediately Ahmed and Mati jumped onto

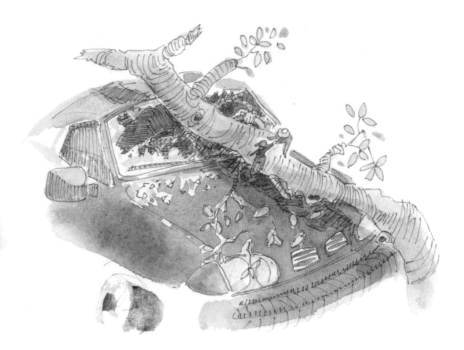

the tree and quickly climbed hand over hand high enough to leap onto the broken branch that had fallen on the front end of the car. The branch lay near the open window. The boys scrambled along the branch and were able to reach the open window. Without a second thought, they slipped into the car.

The woman was conscious, but in much pain.

"We're here to help you!" Mati said. "We saw the accident."

The woman had never seen two boys the size of a thumb, but she was so glad that they had come. "I am hurt. I can't move my legs and I am so dizzy. Can you call for more help?"

"Do you have a cell phone?" Ahmed blurted out.

"Yes, it's in my purse on the floor."

Immediately the two boys slipped to the floor, found the purse, managed to open it, and there was the cell phone!

Between the two of them they carried the phone up to the seat beside the woman.

"I can dial the emergency number," both boys said almost in unison.

"I'll do '#1', then you do '#0', and I'll do '#1' again," Mati said to Ahmed. They knew that dialing "101" was the way to call for help.

Standing on the phone, Mati and Ahmed pressed the keys with their feet, one after the other.

In a moment, the operator answered.

The boys quickly told the story of the accident, and then they asked for an ambulance to be sent.

"Thank you," the operator said, praising them. "Help is on the way! Stay where you are until the ambulance arrives."

It seemed but a moment when they heard a siren growing louder and louder. The ambulance was soon alongside the car.

Quickly the driver and emergency workers jumped out and managed to pry open the door and free the woman from her damaged car. She was carefully placed on a stretcher.

As she was being carried to the ambulance, she smiled at Mati and Ahmed. "You saved my life!"

"*Refuah shlemah*! Get well soon!" Mati called out to her.

"*Yashfi bsre*! Heal quickly!" Ahmed added. Both boys waved to her until the door to the ambulance was closed.

The two boys looked at each other, not knowing what to say. They had just learned about saving a life, and suddenly they had a big chance to help someone!

Back at Ahmed's home, they told the story to Ahmed's *um* about how they each learned something about saving a life in school and then went out and had a chance to actually do this!

"I am so proud of you boys!" she said.

She then was quiet, thinking. "Do you see how *Torah* and the *Quran* can both still teach us today?!" Mariam continued, with even a few tears falling from her eyes. "Some people never have a chance to help the way you two helped that poor woman."

"Awesome," replied Mati, Ahmed nodding his head. The boys couldn't help smiling.

∼ REPAINTING THE DOORWAY ∼
AFTER HAJJ

There was lots of excitement in Ahmed's home. His father had just returned from the trip of a lifetime, the *Hajj*! It was the trip that every Muslim dreamed of doing, traveling to Mecca, the center of Islam. Millions of people from everywhere in the world meet in Mecca to pray, to learn, and to deepen their faith. Imagine walking, praying and meeting with millions of people!!

Ahmed hoped to go one day himself; but, for now, he was so happy that his father had gone and so eager to hear his stories. In fact, his 'ab even changed his name to Khalil al Hajji in honor of his trip!

The family gathered around Ahmed's 'ab and hung on every word.

"I was amazed at how many people had come," Khalil began. "There were people of every color, speaking so many languages. Some were rich, but some were very poor. We were all dressed alike, very simple clothes. And even if we could not speak in the same language, we became friends by walking together, smiling at each other, and making room for everyone."

"Were there people who couldn't walk?" Ahmed's *um* asked.

"Yes," answered Khalil, "Lots of people used canes and wheelchairs, and everyone made room for them and helped push them along the path."

"It was especially interesting when we walked around the *Kaaba* seven times!" he continued. "It is a very big building covered in black cloth built long ago. It's in the shape of a square. Imagine walking around with so many people, all Muslims!! I must admit I felt a little dizzy!"

Ahmed was so excited. To welcome his father home, he had a secret plan. He knew that some people painted the front door of their home bright green as a clear sign that someone inside had completed the *hajj*. Everyone in the neighborhood would know!

"Hi, Mati," Ahmed said excitedly over the phone. "My *'ab* just returned home from Mecca. It was an amazing trip. It's called going on the *hajj*. Would you help me do something special for him?"

"Yes," Mati responded. "What can I do to help?"

Ahmed could hardly get the words out of his mouth quickly enough. "Sometimes people paint the front door green when someone returns from the *hajj*. I'd like to do this to surprise my *'ab*."

Ahmed knew that Mati had just helped his parents paint in his home. Being the size of a thumb, he could use his tiny paint brush to get into corners that were tough for his parents to do. And he had even gone shopping with his *abba* for the paint.

"Yes," Mati said excitedly. "This sounds like fun."

That very day the two boys met in the center of Jerusalem. They walked into the paint store together.

"Do you have bright green paint?" asked Ahmed.

"Of course we do!" answered the clerk, peering down over the counter where the two tiny boys stood. Looking at Mati, he said, "I remember you. You came in standing on your *abba's* shoulder recently."

"Yes, I did." Mati said.

"It isn't everyday that thumb-sized boys come in. And now there are two!"

The clerk showed the boys several shades of green.

"I like the brightest," announced Ahmed. "My 'ab just came back from the *hajj!*"

"Ahhh," said the clerk, "Now I understand. This is for the front door of your house, isn't it? So, this is the best color green you could choose!"

"Can you deliver it to my house," asked Ahmed. "And can you send the paint in your smallest cans with two of your smallest brushes?"

"Yes, they will arrive by this afternoon," the clerk declared.

The very next day, soon after Khalil had left for work, Mati rode his bike to Ahmed's home. He had his old clothes on, and he was ready to work. If they wanted to complete Ahmed's surprise before his father came home, they had to work fast. In fact, no one was home since Ahmed's *um* had gone to work too. This was Ahmed's surprise for the whole family.

Mati helped Ahmed carry a ladder and placed it next to the door. It was lightweight with tiny steps to climb, but it could be extended to reach very high.

"Let's start at the top," suggested Ahmed. "We can work our way down."

"I can't wait to get going," replied Mati.

Up they went to the very top of the door carrying the paint in two small cans, their brushes, and even some tape. It was a long way up, and the two boys were breathing hard as they struggled to reach the top. Now they stood together on a very high rung.

The day was beautiful with the sun shining in a blue sky with very little breeze. It was a perfect day for painting. Immediately the boys set to work by covering the wood frame around the door with tape so that the green paint would only remain on the door. Then they stirred the paint until it looked perfect.

"Here we go," Ahmed called out happily, as he dipped his brush into the very green paint. He made a few strokes, looked at Mati, and declared: "Look at this! *Abi* will be so proud!"

Mati took hold of his brush and set to work. The door had originally been painted white. Now the bright green paint really stood out. "This is fun!" Mati called out.

Mati climbed down one rung so that they would have more room to work. It is hard to paint without dripping, and soon Ahmed's brush sent drops down onto Mati's hair.

The drops were so tiny that neither of the boys even noticed. The boys alternated being one rung higher than the other as they continued to paint. Soon, Ahmed's hair was also pelted with drops from Mati's brush. They didn't even notice because they were so intent on finishing the door. If only their hair turned green it would have been enough. But before they knew it, both boys looked like green Martians! There was as much paint on them as on the door!

They looked at each other and laughed. "You, too, must have been on the *hajj!*" Mati joked.

"And you must have gone on the *hajj!*" Ahmed laughed. "Your *kippah* is now green!"

Finally, after hours had passed, the two boys stood on the ground admiring a perfectly green door.

"We have to get cleaned up before my parents

come home," Ahmed declared. "Then you can borrow some of my clean clothes."

Ahmed turned on the water in his special tiny bathtub and invited Mati to jump in before he, too, took his turn. Soon they were both clean, but there was a big green ring around the tub!

"What can we do about that?" asked Mati.

"Here's an old towel we can use." Ahmed said.

The boys scrubbed the tub with the towel, and the paint was gone; but now the towel was bright green!

"We can do a load of wash with the towel," said Ahmed, as he quickly added the towel to other clothes in the washing machine and, standing on a chair, pushed the button to turn it on.

Were the boys ever surprised when everything came out green!

"Oh, no!!" gasped Ahmed. "What will *ummi* say when she sees her white blouse has turned green?!"

At that moment, a car pulled up with Ahmed's parents. Mati and Ahmed rushed outside to meet them.

"Don't touch the door!" Ahmed called out. "It's wet paint!"

Ahmed's parents were speechless.

"I wanted to surprise you, *Abi*," blurted out Ahmed. "Mati came to help."

"Wow!! You did this all by yourselves. Amazing!" Khalil said. "How can I thank you two boys?! And what a good job you did painting. It looks professional!"

"We want everyone to know what you did," Ahmed said.

"We had fun painting the door," added Mati.

Later on, when Ahmed's parents saw the pile of newly washed green clothes, his *um* declared: "Green is now the official color of our family. From now on, I will wear green to show how proud I am of my husband! And you, Ahmed, will wear green underwear and green socks!!"

∽ BROADCASTING THE MIRACLE ∽
OF CHANUKAH

The eighth night of *Chanukah* is the most exciting because all the candles on the *Chanukiah* are burning. The home is filled with candle light. It is even more so when that last night coincides with *Shabbat* and even more candles are lit!

Ahmed was a guest at Mati's home for the lighting of all eight candles and a great feast. The entire family was watching by the large front window. After singing blessings in Hebrew, Mati stood on his *abba's* hand

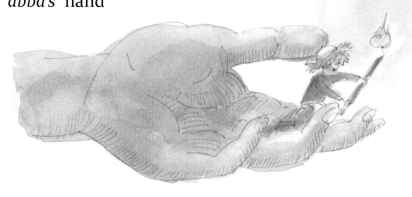

holding a candle which was almost as big as he was! He carefully reached out to light the wick on each candle.

"Those eight candles are so beautiful," Ahmed exclaimed, as he counted them lined up in a row. "Why do you light so many?"

"A long time ago, when the big Temple stood in Jerusalem, the *Maccabees* wanted to light the flame that was supposed to burn all the time," Mati's *abba* answered. "They used pure olive oil, and they only had enough for one day. But the oil burned for eight days until more could be found. A miracle!"

"Wow! That *is* a miracle," Ahmed added. "Can't miss seeing the lights when someone passes by your window!"

"We're supposed to let everyone know," quipped Mati. "That's why we light by the window."

"Are we going to stand here all night?" asked Mati's *imma*. "You are invited to come to the table for a *Shabbat Chanukah* dinner."

Everyone was hungry, and the fragrance of the meal lured everyone quickly to take their seats. Mati sat next to Ahmed on two very high booster seats. Blessings were said over the grape juice and the delicious *challah* bread.

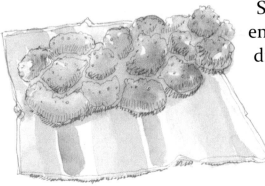

Soon everyone was enjoying the festive dinner of chicken, potato kugel, and a fresh vegetable salad.

After dinner, the boys took turns spinning a tiny *dreidel,* a top especially used on *Chanukah.* Ahmed became an expert with the *dreidel.*

It had been a long evening, and Mati and Ahmed were tired and thirsty.

"Ahmed, I know where we can get a drink. From the *Kiddush* cup we used at dinner!" Mati suggested. "There's always some grape juice left over in the cup."

The large cup had been placed on the window sill next to the still burning *chanukiah.* The window was opened a bit, too, to allow a breeze to enter. A chair was next to the window, and soon the boys were climbing up the back of the chair until they reached the window sill. The cup was made of glass, tall, and beautiful.

"Follow me!" Mati told Ahmed. He wrapped his

legs around the base of the cup and up he climbed with Ahmed just behind him. Soon they had reached the top of the cup and peered in. Sure enough, they saw that there was grape juice!

Mati and Ahmed looked at each other with a grin, climbed over the top of the cup and tried to reach down to the juice to drink. Their feet hung onto the top rim of the cup. But they didn't realize until it was too late that their weight on one side of the cup was too much! The *kiddush* cup began to tip over! Oh, no!

There was nothing they could do but to hold onto each other to avoid falling out of the cup. The inside of the cup was also sticky from the grape juice.

The *kiddush* cup fell towards the *chanukiah*; and it, too, began to tip over with all of the candles ablaze! The bottom of the cup touched the base of the *chanukiah*. Around the base melted wax from the candles had dripped. Suddenly the sticky juice and the wax mixed together. The cup was now tightly stuck to the *chanukiah*!

The burning flames became like eight jet engines! And the *kiddush* cup/*chanukiah* began to shake. Inside the cup Mati and Ahmed were frightened, and they clung to each other. They felt that they were moving! This strange contraption began to slowly lift off the window sill through the open window and into the dark night sky! Higher and higher the boys flew. Only now did they realize that they were in a unique spacecraft! And, below, people began to look up, point to the sky, and wonder if this was the new miracle of *Chanukah*.

Mati and Ahmed had never been in space before. At first it was scary, but soon the two boys figured out that they had to quickly learn how to guide their spacecraft so that they could have a safe landing! Looking through the glass in their "cockpit", they soon noticed that by moving themselves this way and that way, they could actually steer their craft. They flew back and forth in the sky over the neighborhood where Mati lived and even over the neighborhood where Ahmed's home stood.

"I can see my street and my house!" exclaimed Ahmed.

"Yes, and your family can see us if they are looking up!" said Mati.

Everywhere people did stop, look up, and point.

"What is that??" one woman asked. "Is it a spaceship?"

"It looks like candles burning!" another said. "I can count eight!"

"I can't believe my eyes!" exclaimed a man out loud. "I think it's a *chanukiah!*"

It wasn't long before the candles burned low, and this unusual spacecraft flew lower and lower. Mati and Ahmed had to think fast. They had to avoid a crash!

"Come closer to me, Ahmed," said Mati. "I see my home ahead! Let's try to land there!"

It was tense in the cockpit. Now they were very low, headed for the ground. Before them was Mati's home, then the window which was still open.

The boys wrapped their arms around each other, moved quickly to one side to aim their spacecraft towards the open window.

"Hold on!" Ahmed screamed.

The sudden impact on the windowsill caused the *kiddush* cup and the *chanukiah* to break apart. The boys tumbled out of the cup. They were sticky, covered with grape juice and with melted wax.

The sound of the crash brought Mati's parents running into the room.

"What have you been up to?" sighed Mati's *imma*, seeing the mess the boys had made. The *chanukiah* and the *kiddush* cup lay on their sides. Melted wax and grape juice covered the windowsill and the boys.

"We...we...we flew through the air," stammered Mati, knowing that his parents would not believe him.

"Boys will be boys!" *Imma* sighed.

"Let's get you cleaned up so I can take Ahmed home," said *Abba*.

The next morning at breakfast in two homes, Mati and Ahmed's parents sat reading the morning newspaper. They were so very surprised at the headlines: **"Strange Chanukiah Sighted in the Sky Over Jerusalem!"**

"I've never seen such a sight!" said Ahmed's *ab* to his wife and to him. "Have you?"

Ahmed smiled and nodded.

"This sounds to me like still another miracle! Never has the story of *Chanukah* been broadcast so far!" Mati's *imma* said.

Mati could not even begin to explain.

One more adventure . . .

～ VISITING NEVE SHALOM ～ WAHAT AL SALAAM

"Would you like to go on a trip?" Mati asked Ahmed.

"Where to?" Ahmed answered with a question of his own.

"My class has been invited to *Neve Shalom Wahat Al Salaam*," Mati answered. "It's a place on the way to Tel Aviv where Jews, Muslims, and Christians live and learn together. We will play games and learn about each other. I hear it's fun there!"

"Do you think that my class could go, too?"

"Let's ask. It's a place for Muslims, too!"

Soon it was arranged. Mati's class and Ahmed's class sat together on a big bus. Of course, the two thumb-sized boys sat together on one seat.

The ride was exciting, passing fields filled with wild flowers on this spring day. Was any color missing from the huge display of flowers? As far as their eyes could see, there was a blanket of red, purple, yellow, white and blue.

Hearing the excitement of the kids on the bus, the bus driver checked with the teachers and pulled his bus over to the side of the road.

One teacher announced over the loudspeaker system. "Would you like to pick bouquets of flowers to take with us? We can bring a gift for the people at *Neve Shalom!*"

"Yes, yes!!" the students shouted.

The students, with Mati and Ahmed among them, quickly jumped out the door of the bus and scattered among the flowers. The flowers grew high above Mati and Ahmed's heads, and the boys soon disappeared among them. They were determined to gather flowers, too.

"Mati, climb up on my shoulders," Ahmed urged. "Then you can see the colors, and we won't miss any of them."

"Here I go!" Mati answered. Ahmed bent over, and soon Mati stood on his shoulders.

Mati called down instructions to Ahmed which flowers to pick. Very soon they had a beautiful bouquet. When they were finished choosing, Ahmed bent down once again, and Mati jumped onto the ground. With Ahmed holding the stems and Mati wrapping his arms around the flowers, they carried their bouquet onto the bus.

Once on their way again, Mati's teacher once again picked up her microphone: "Let's sing! I will teach you the words."

She immediately began: "*Hineh mah tov u'mah na-im, she-vet ah-chim gam yah'chad!*" "*How good and pleasant it is for brothers (and sisters) to live together!*"

Ahmed had heard the song before, but he did not know it by heart like some of the Jewish kids. Soon he and his classmates were singing loudly along with everyone. They spoke Hebrew very well.

Singing made the time pass quickly. Soon, in the distance, set upon a hill, they saw Neve Shalom. It looked beautiful with mostly white buildings set among green leafy trees. Even from a distance they could pick out the Hall of Silence, an unusually shaped building where people could pray in their own ways.

When they arrived, they were greeted with big smiles by adults and other kids and shown around the site. They visited the school where kids their own age studied together. They were especially excited to see the playground nearby. At its entrance, they walked under a large rainbow made of plastic pipes. Atop the rainbow, Ahmed and Mati saw a sculpture of a dove, which seemed about to fly.

In the village, everyone was excited because three holidays were coming soon, all at the same time! Passover, Easter, and Ramadan. Jews, Christians, and Muslims would all have special days to celebrate. In the school, the teachers wanted their students to know about these holidays. Mati and Ahmed and their classes were invited to take part.

Each student was asked to find another who belonged to a different religion. Of course, Mati and Ahmed, the only thumb-sized kids, were a natural pair. Together with the other kids they learned about each holiday.

"This is an amazing time," said a teacher. "All of us will have holidays at the same time! But each one is different. Who can tell us about Passover?"

Many hands went up, and the teacher pointed to one girl.

"It's about the Jews being rescued from slavery and going free," she said. "We have a great meal with *matzah*, very flat bread, and tell the story of how it happened."

"Perfect," said the teacher. "And who can tell us something about Easter?"

More hands went up, and a boy answered: "Easter is a very happy holiday where we remember how Jesus was alive after everyone thought he had died!"

"And what about Ramadan?" the teacher asked.

"It's a whole month where grown-ups do not eat during the day but have special meals at night. We try hard to be better people!" another student answered.

"Good start, everyone," said the teacher. "Now we will go from station to station to learn more about each holiday and each other."

At the end, each pair of students
was asked to prepare a skit, write
a song, or anything else
to present to the
other students
what they had
learned. Ahmed
and Mati were the
first to volunteer.
They stepped
forward and began to rap!

For all of us it's such a boon

To have a holiday coming soon

In every synagogue, church, and mosque,

People have this happy task

To rejoice in their own way.

To fast or eat or sing or pray.

Mati: "In my house, our family sits

Telling how Pharoah gave us fits.

Then God took slaves and made them free.

We tell this story with much glee!"

Ahmed: "We fast by day and eat by night

For one whole month, it takes some might!

When I fast, I realize

 I can be better, even at my size!"

Mati and Ahmed together:

"We learned that Easter is a day of joy

A day of hope, not a day to cry

As the sun rises, some climb up high

To bless God under the fresh, blue sky!

We've learned so much, and now we say

We like knowing kids with a different way

This world of ours just seems better

When we can all be different together!"

All the kids applauded at the sight and sound of two tiny boys rapping together.

To finish the day, one of the guides from Neve Shalom led the group to the building called *Hechal Ha-Doumia V'Sakhina, The Hall of Silence and Peacefulness.*

At the entrance, the guide said: "We are about to enter a special place. We won't talk once we go inside.

But we can each thank God in our own ways for being together today, for new friends, for everything that we share and for everything that is different, too."

Inside this beautiful building, everyone, Jewish, Christian, and Muslim people, stood, sat, or bowed down alongside each other.

Mati and Ahmed were amazed. It felt good to be different together.

∽ ACKNOWLEDGEMENTS ∽

I am filled with gratitude for the generosity of so many who have helped me bring this work to fruition. Truly I feel I am attached to a network of partners/ supporters who encouraged me and affirmed that these stories were worthy of publication.

I am very thankful to my willing readers, Theda Firschein and Karen Huberman, distinguished authors and lovers of children's literature, whose wise, thoughtful comments made me think, edit, and recast many passages. Betty Fellows, my faithful partner in so many enterprises, once again has generously helped to format these stories. My dear friend, mentor, and decades-long partner in interfaith dialogue, Rev. Doug Huneke, is ever willing to remind me to "show, not tell". He is always cheerleading for me!

My chevruta, study partner, Atara Moalem, gifted teacher of young people, has not only read my stories but beta tested some of them with her students. She knows the pain of the Israeli-Arab conflict first-hand, and she shares my dream of open heartedness and reconciliation.

My editor at Hadassa Word Press, Elena Djima,

would be any author's dream of a partner in publishing. She and the Press have been willing to stretch to enter the world of children's literature and to make room for colored illustrations to enhance the reader's experience. Elena is ever positive, always timely in her communications, and helpful in too many ways to describe.

My stories are lifted off the page by Kim Howard, my treasured illustrator. She was able immediately to capture the spirit of the these two miniature kids and to make them come alive in ways that I could not envision. This is "our book", truly a partnership. As she has befriended these tiny boys, she has become a trusted friend to me as well.

When I first began to write for children, I hoped that my granddaughter, Sari Lewis, would emerge as an illustrator for my books! She is a gifted, emerging artist. And I am so pleased that she contributed two images for these stories. I love her work.

My illustrator is Christian, and it means so much to me that, once again, the designer of this sequel volume is a Muslim woman, Rashida Basrai. Her work is always meticulous, caring, and aesthetically pleasing. How blessed I am to be able to claim that this work is a collaboration of three faiths!

I must admit that I use my grandchildren

shamelessly to test some of my stories. They come along willingly, and, at times, to my joy, ask that I repeat a story! What would I do without having them to catalyze my imagination?!

My wife, Lorri, is my silent partner in all of my work. She provides the stability, tranquility, and support I need to be creative. How blessed I am to have shared our lives for 47 plus years!

I am eternally grateful to God for enabling me to reach this day.